CABBAGE

Copyright © 2023 by C.S. Fritz

All rights reserved. No part of this publication may be reproduced, distributed, or transmitted in any form or by any means, including photocopying, recording, digital scanning, or other electronic or mechanical methods, without the prior written permission of the publisher, except in the case of brief quotations embodied in critical reviews and certain other noncommercial uses permitted by copyright law. For permission requests, visit and contact the publisher through the website listed below.

ISBN (paperback): 978-1-959153-10-8
ISBN (eBook): 978-1-959153-11-5

This is a work of fiction. Names, places, characters and incidents are either the product of the author's imagination or are used fictitiously, and any resemblance to any actual persons, living or dead, organizations, events or locales is entirely coincidental.

Printed in the United States of America.

Published by

ALBATROSS BOOK CO.

www.albatrossbookco.com

CABBAGE

A SHORT STORY

C.S. FRITZ

Enjoy this author-curated playlist as you read.

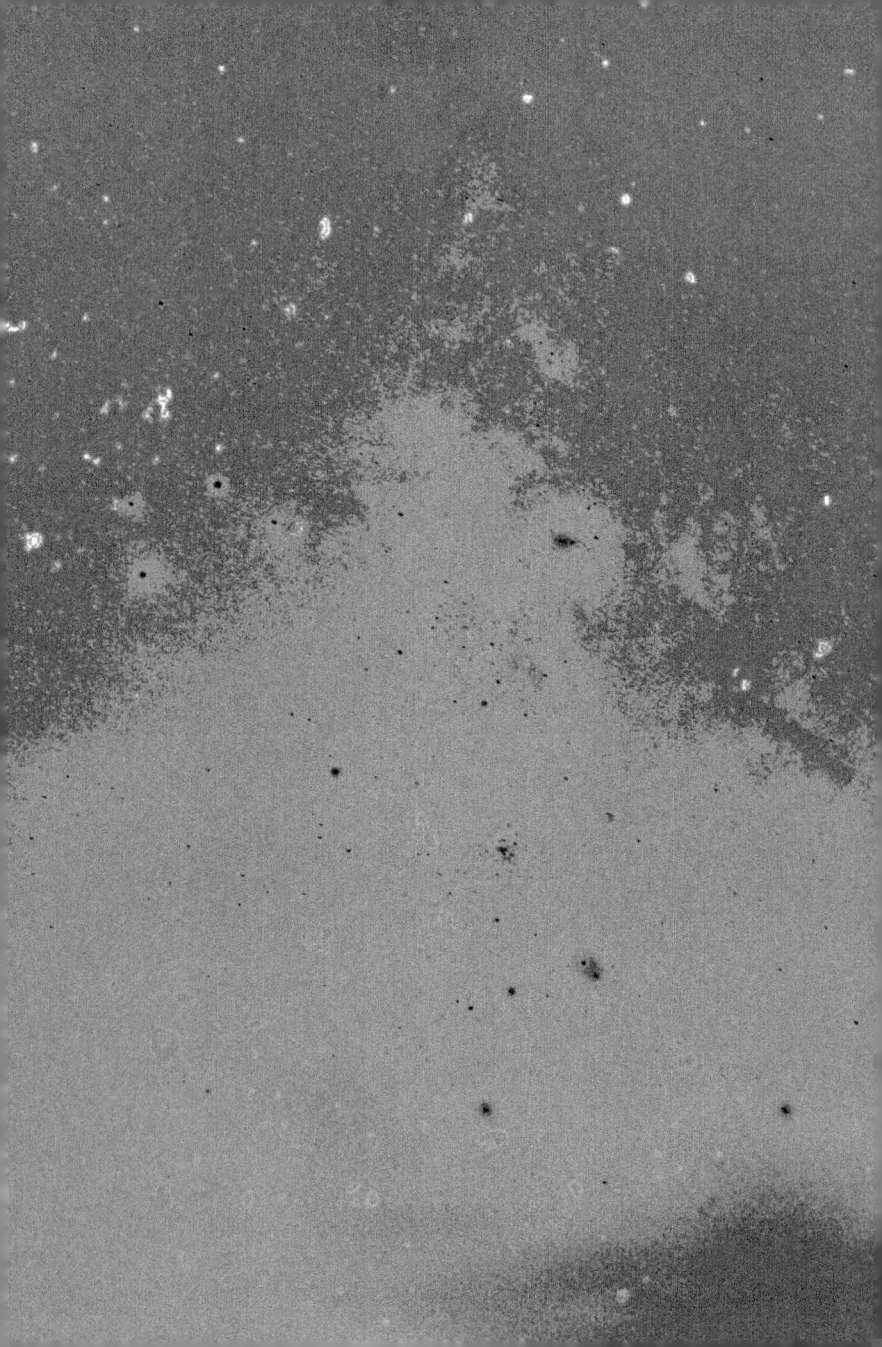

*For Lorenzo,
an undeserved friend,
true partner, and beloved brother.*

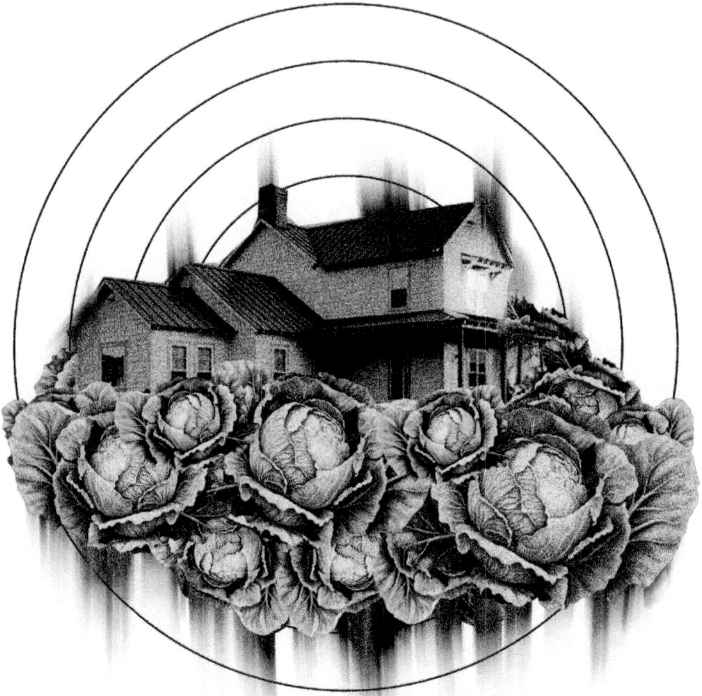

I went to the Garden of Love,
And saw what I never had seen;
A Chapel was built in the midst,
Where I used to play on the green.
And the gates of this Chapel were shut,
And 'Thou shalt not' writ over the door;
So I turned to the Garden of Love
That so many sweet flowers bore.

And I saw it was filled with graves,
And tombstones where flowers should be;
And priests in black gowns were walking their rounds,
And binding with briars my joys and desires.

- William Blake

Verily, verily, I say unto you, Except a grain of wheat fall into the earth and die, it abideth by itself alone; but if it die, it beareth much fruit. He that loveth his life loseth it; and he that hateth his life in this world shall keep it unto life eternal.

John 12:24

Thomas handed his wife a small mason jar. Inside, thousands of hardened unborn shook and rattled against the sides of the glass . . .

"Thomas! You found them!" Rosemary exclaimed.

"I did. Nearly every rose and head of cabbage here came from these seeds. Your seeds."

Rosemary grabbed her husband's calloused hands, kissed them in gratitude, and returned to examining her newly found treasure. Thomas loved to see her happy, but it was her smiles that were now worth more than all of the world's gold.

"It took months, but what else was I going to do while you were in the hospital?" He said with a chuckle.

"Thank you my love. My father would be very proud to see his farm continue on like this. That I'm sure of."

"Well, your happiness is my aim, Dear," Thomas replied with a grin, "Now, let me show you what else I've been up to . . . but first, I need to blindfold you."

"Oh, Thomas, you're too much." Rosemary said with a giddiness he hadn't seen in ages. She continued to grasp the jar of differing seeds, grains, and nuts tightly. He wrapped his wife's eyes with his old, weathered farmer's bandana and maneuvered around her wheelchair, escorting her outside to the garden.

"You ready, my love?" The old man asked, removing the bandana from Rosemary's eyes. He then

CABBAGE

promptly gestured like a magician revealing a trick might. "Tada!" he exclaimed.

Rosemary instinctively blocked her eyes from the evening sun, which colored her face white and let her aging eyes adjust to the new landscape. With two hands resting on her eyebrows, she squinted and could see what her Thomas had been working on so faithfully since the diagnosis—the garden of her dreams. The garden from her childhood, from another life lived. Rosemary gasped as Thomas hoped she would, and he let out his sigh of relief, folding his bandana and putting it back into his overall pockets.

Bending down to her level he whispered, "Will it do my Dear? So that . . . well, you know."

Rosemary's mouth was now cupped by her hands, which was all the assurance he needed that this would be the perfect place for his wife of fifty-three years to live out her remaining days. Rosemary then grabbed Thomas's hand, as he placed the other on top of hers, the feeling of the medical tape and tubing which sprung from it like Cypress Vine a constant reminder of their very reality.

"Come, no more talk of that. Show me around," Rosemary said, patting Thomas's shaky hands like an encouraging priest and attempting to maneuver her chair towards her gift. Thomas carefully gave her wheelchair a good shove to get them on top of the brick pavers with his left hand, while steadying the medical

CABBAGE

pole which held his wife's vitals in his right. "Here I planted the Marigolds," Thomas said softly, pointing. "Do you remember?" he asked.

"Of course I remember. They were the same flowers you brought home to me on the day our daughter was born," Rosemary said. "Thank you for that."

They continued down the path, Thomas struggling here and there with his own limitations, but he knew nothing would stop him from this most important journey. "And here are your Gayfeathers, Easter Lilies, and Ladybells."

"Oh! It's just like my bouquet from our wedding! How did you remember?" Rosemary exclaimed. "Lucky guess," he said, with a wink. "And finally, cabbage, your favorite." To which Rosemary quite uncontrollably blurted out with a loud honk of laughter, "Oh my stars! More like *your* favorite if I remember correctly."

"Should we recreate that night?"

"Thomas!" Rosemary blushed, "There would be nothing I would enjoy more, *if I could.*"

"I know my Dear, I know." Thomas said, allowing the words to go from sweet to sour. Normally he wouldn't allow her thoughts to traverse into what they both knew lurked just beyond their every waking thought. Especially here. He wanted this garden to be a place of solace. Of peace. A small shred of what joy they may have left in this life that seemed to leave deeper scars than laugh lines. But sometimes the reality of their

CABBAGE

situation was too bleak, and in a bizarre way, letting it come to the surface every now and then was a needed release. The two stayed there in silence, allowing the sun to kiss them goodnight as it sank into the horizon. *Another day gone,* the old man thought.

Rosemary lifted the jar, and gave it another gentle shake, cooing at the seeds like one might to a pet or a child.

"Do you think the seeds know they must die?"

"What?" Thomas asked, suddenly torn from his own thoughts, shocked by the sudden mood change. "What do you mean?"

Rosemary tilted the jar and examined it closer, not looking up at her bewildered husband. "Do you think the seed *knows* it must die, so that greater life will live on?" she asked again, unafraid to wonder.

But, before Thomas could answer, Rosemary let out a cough. *That* cough. The cough that alerted them some time ago to the disease. She reached back to Thomas for a place to steady herself, gripping her hands onto his. "I think I should go in for a few."

"Of course." Thomas said wearily, but could feel shadows of disappointment growing within him. In fact, these were feelings he'd been harboring for some time now. Disappointment, like an infant growing within that he wished he could abort. Disappointment with the God above, the endless medical professionals, testing, medications and misdiagnoses sucking his

CABBAGE

retirement savings dry, all leading to the same result; "There is no cure. There's nothing we can do." But most of all, disappointment with his one true love, and the life they could have had. That was robbed of him. Of her. Dismantling those expectations and replacing them with bricks of mercy was his new mode of existence, and he hated the deepest parts of the cosmos for it. "It's time for your blood work anyways; I'll put a kettle on for tea as well, and we'll finish watching the sun go down."

"That sounds great Dear," Rosemary said as she let the Milk Thistle gingerly fondle her furrowed fingers, while Thomas pulled the chair toward the back door of their humble cottage. Rosemary kept her eyes on the new green horizon, admiring her husband's work. From the soft, buttery yellow details of Lady's Mantle to the richly green and pointed leaves of the Lemon Cucumber that spilled over the edges of the boxes. Beyond, she could see the faint outline of the Licorice plant heating up in the dying sunlight, the delicate Linseeds, Bluestems and robust Lungwort. Each held a differing memorial place, both in the soil and their collected memories in her mind. Rosemary's heart was bursting with gratitude for her enduring husband's care and thoughtfulness. But, like crabgrass which strangles the earth, suffocating the beauty from the inside out, Rosemary, in her bliss, sat confined to her chair, knowing the next time she'd step into her garden, it'd probably be for her own burial.

CABBAGE

Thomas rubbed his fingers in the arm crevice of Rosemary's spoiled skin, searching like a bloodhound for the antecubital fossa. He wiped the alcohol swab gently between her bruises and browning spots. He had only done this a few times before, and his nerves still got the best of him. Needles were not his forte, and if he thought about it long enough, would make him weak in the knees. But, it was either this or not at all, due to the lack of insurance and funds to pay for the live-in nurse they so desperately needed. Rosemary listened as Thomas whispered carefully and methodically the steps to himself, dragging the bedside lamp closer for more light. "Tourniquet-beveled needle at a 30-degree angle into the vessel—connect the vacutainers, then label," he rehearsed.

"Very good, Love." Rosemary whispered, as she looked away. The sight of blood had had stronger effects on her since discovering the cancer.

"I believe I'm getting the hang of it now," the old man said excitedly, as the thick, purple life was drawn from his dying wife into the collection bag.

Rosemary smiled, but Thomas would never have seen it, as it wasn't for him. That smile was for her—Rosemary, with her imminence, had been trying to collect moments—Thomas moments, better moments. Stowing them like fireflies in her heart as if it was a faunarium. Firefly thoughts of Thomas asking the cat every morning what he wanted for breakfast, but then apologizing for being out of Raspberry Pain

CABBAGE

au Chocolat. Or how every time Thomas bent over, the world was greeted with a dawning of Thomas' shrinking behind and its slender crack. She needed these moments to replace the others; to put roses where thorns had been.

"There!" He exclaimed, sealing the clear blood sack and placing it on the table nearby. "Now, what do you want for dinner?"

"Spezzatino di Manzo, please!" Rosemary said with a wide grin.

"Ha! I'll get right on that *Signora*."

"Do you remember when we had that for the first time?" Rosemary said, grabbing his arm, to not let him leave.

"Of course, in that villa outside of Portofino."

"Yes!" Rosemary said loudly. "God, it was the best stew of my life."

"I don't even like stew, but that was heavenly. I know it's not Spezzatino di Manzo, but how does cabbage soup sound?" He asked with broken eyes.

"That'll do," she replied, with a blend of disappointment and contentedness all rolled into one.

"Good," Thomas said, patting Rosemary's soft hand. "I left the cooler in the car from this morning's hospital run; I'll be back in a flash with your soup. In the meantime, Google a cure for stage four pancreatic cancer, will ya?"

"On it!" Rosemary said with a forced chuckle.

CABBAGE

Thomas turned on the porch light and made his way toward their old pick-up, with the blood sack in hand. He was chuckling to himself at the absurdity of his own joke, as the crickets played their songs. Above, the moonlight lit his path. Bright, navigating stars and warm summer breezes still gave him much to be grateful for. Stopping on his way to harvest some cabbage to boil for Rosemary, something unexpected happened. Something so terrible, even the crickets stopped to listen. Thomas watched as if in slow motion as his wife's blood broke through its adhesive dam and poured itself into the cabbage patch, turning it a deep purple. "Fuck me!" Thomas squealed, quickly cupping his mouth so as to not alert Rosemary to his mistake.

Thomas didn't dare think about the last time he saw blood in his field, forcing his mind to go black to that moment. Begging the demon memory to be merciful. But then, in a flash, he grabbed the watering can to spray down her precious blood into the soil below. Knowing he could never tell Rosemary; not another accident in the garden. Or she'd beg him to go back into hospice and allow the nurses there to take care of all this messy work. But he knew all too well they couldn't afford that kind of care, nor did he want her in a place like that . . . Instead, he grabbed the cooler and threw the empty sack away, burying it beneath earlier garbage. He meandered back inside, letting the screen door crack behind him like a whip, trying to conceal his labored breathing.

CABBAGE

"On second thought," he shouted into the other room, "how does spaghetti sound?"

"That's great, Dear!" Rosemary exclaimed.

Thomas prepared the water for boil, staring out their kitchen window into his newly planted garden beneath the moon. Unaware of the horrors that he had just unleashed.

*O Master of the Garden,
O my sun and rain and dew,
Come quickly.*

Helen Hoyt

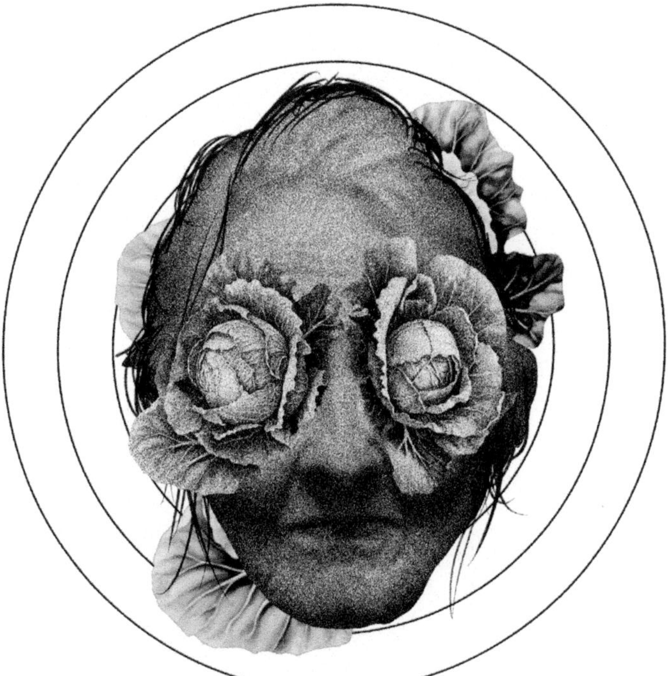

Thomas reached into each of the individual chicken slots, patting the straw gently for any sign of eggs. Basket in hand, he patiently went to each opening as if it were an easter hunt. "You girls just don't seem to wanna help me out, do you?" Thomas asked, setting himself down upon the barn's dusty floor and lighting a cigarette.

Drip

"Come here, girl," Thomas whispered, with the cigarette pushed to one side of mouth. He placed one of his Andalusians on his lap. Since Rosemary's diagnosis, Thomas found himself in the barn more and more, not necessarily working or cleaning, but just staring. Allowing his eyes to be still and unfocused. He enjoyed the blur of the world around him, as it made him feel, if only for a moment . . . unseen.

Drip

Minutes without blinking, frosting his eyes in the thick barnyard air. Long drags between breaths. The chickens, soon bored and realizing no snacks were coming, long since wandered off.

Drip

Allowing his mind and lungs to darken, before another troubled day filled itself with Bendamustine, Dabrafenib, and Herceptin. Like a capsule in deep space, this was his only moment of emotional stillness before impact. He needed that stillness. He needed—

Drip

CABBAGE

"Fuck me!" Thomas said beneath his dragon breath, as the dripping sound infiltrated his thoughts. Glancing outward to the piercing canons of whatever was dripping in his garden, he marched outside to obliterate whatever had the audacity to disturb his one, singular moment of peace. But what Thomas saw was nearly impossible to put into words; not that it was indescribable, but that it was just *impossible*. Like angel flesh, or a map to Neverland. Thomas watched as thick and dark purple blood dripped from his cabbage plants' leaves and stems into a pool of their own making, collected on the soil. Each cultivar, sculpted and shaped, was unnaturally forming leaf pockets and tendrils that reached upwards, almost as if to grab Thomas.

It was the smell that struck him then. Like an arrow in the head—*Spezzatino di Manzo*. The smell was unmistakable. As Thomas leaned in, he could see the cabbage cultivar was cupping an italian stew. Hot, with a mild boil, as umber bubbles popped themselves over and down the folded cabbage leaves. Thomas, almost instinctively, like a chef might test their creation, stuck his finger in their openings and licked the cabbage-blood substance from its cups.

"Shit on a stick," Thomas muttered. *It couldn't be,* he thought. *How the hell could the stew . . . Wait . . . What the fuck . . .* His mind darted and stung like wasps, trying to make sense of the supernatural. Thomas ran inside and grabbed a wooden bowl, harvesting the stew as quickly as he could.

CABBAGE

"Rosemary!" he shouted, bolting into the house. "You won't believe this."

If heart are gardens,
plant those flowers
in the chest of the ones
who exist around you.

R.H. Swaney

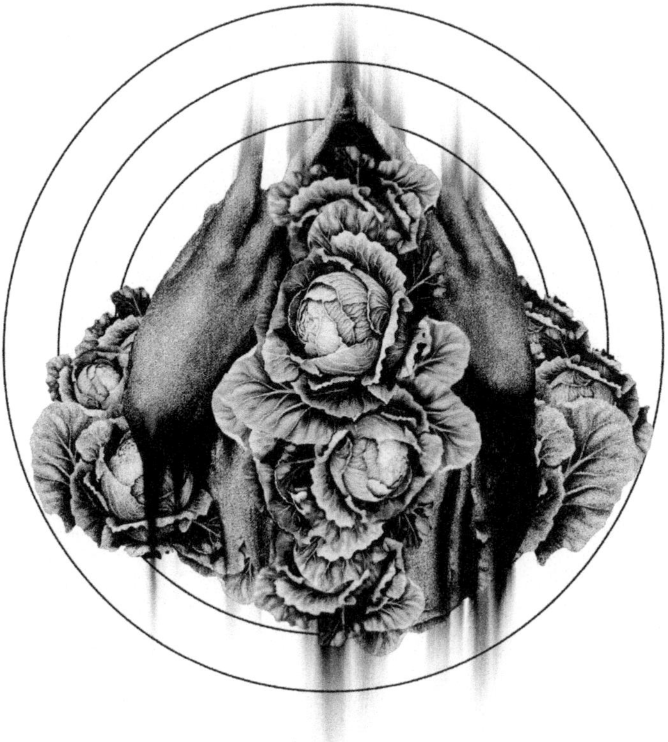

Rosemary drank the stew to its leafy dregs as Thomas watched, biting his nails in bewilderment. "My god that is good," Rosemary said, smacking her salty lips. "But, it's not a *Spezzatino di Manzo.*"

"What do you mean?" Thomas asked, closing the window curtains, the sight of the garden causing a new sense of unease he couldn't put his finger on just yet. Or rather, maybe it was that he felt the garden was . . . *watching* him.

"*Spezzatino di Manzo* has beef. This has eggplant, radish, and beets."

Thomas continued to listen as his brain fought for reality.

"Tell me how it happened again?" she asked with a childish tone.

"I told you, I dropped your blood count bag as I went to grab the fucking–"

"Language, Thomas!"

"Sorry my Dear. I went to grab the cooler and spilled your blood accidentally into the cabbage patch. That's it." Just sharing with Rosemary again about the bloodied accident in the field gave him a shudder.

"It's a miracle then, my Love."

"Why are you so quick to the miraculous?"

"Why aren't you? Haven't we been praying for miracles?"

"For your healing, not for soup."

CABBAGE

"What's the difference? A miracle is a miracle. Do you believe one miracle has more value than another?"

Thomas hated arguing theology with Rosemary, as she often won on the basis of harboring a wilder faith than his own. Something he always envied in his wife. He often reflected on the time she encouraged his own baptism to be done by a priest. But the old farmer was stubborn and had a liking to do things himself. A young Rosemary had watched as her husband nearly drowned himself in the horse trough, hitting the back of his head against its tin curve. Since then, Thomas had kept his theology to himself, as to not be made a fool.

"I have an idea," Rosemary said, readjusting herself and reaching for the vacutainer.

"Don't you dare!" Thomas squawked, shooing his wife's hands away from the nightstand.

"Why not? It's not like the blood is doing me any good; in fact we should dump it all out."

Thomas knew he'd lose this wrestle as well, and decided to give into the drama instead. "Here, let me do it," he said, thinking to himself that this would put to rest her miracle-notion and they could chalk it up to a phenomenon, aliens, or garden gnomes, which felt a lot more palatable than the alternative. Thomas sealed the bag and began his trek to the backyard

"Wait!" Rosemary shouted. "Last night I *wanted* something, I *need* to want," she explained, rubbing her soft chin.

CABBAGE

"Jesus, Rosemary," Thomas replied, waiting in the doorway, bag in hand, wishing it all would end.

"I got it. You may go," his wife said with a confident grin. Thomas was happier to give into this charade than receive any condemnation for the wrongdoing. Plus, there was that smile again.

He pushed the screen door open harder than he normally would, stomped into his fresh soil and located the cabbage. The smell of *Spezzatino di Manzo* still kissed the air, as tiny insects floated like angels near the garden. A very real reminder that what had transpired couldn't be chalked up to a grief-stricken dream or hallucination. Something was here; something was in the soil.

"Double fuck me," Thomas spat under his breath at the sheer ridiculousness of the situation. He took out his overall pocket knife, stabbed the plastic pouch and sprinkled his wife's diseased blood graciously upon the freshly planted cabbage leaves. Once the bag was emptied and the ritual was complete, he threw the bag into the neighboring English tea roses and wiped his hands against his legs. His eyes looked up, as if to catch God watching, peeking from behind the clouds.

"There; now do your thing."

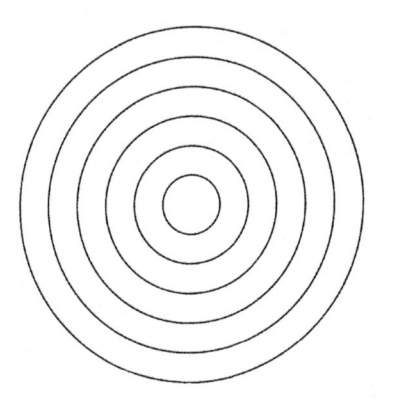

Tread softly because you tread on my dreams

W.B. Yeats

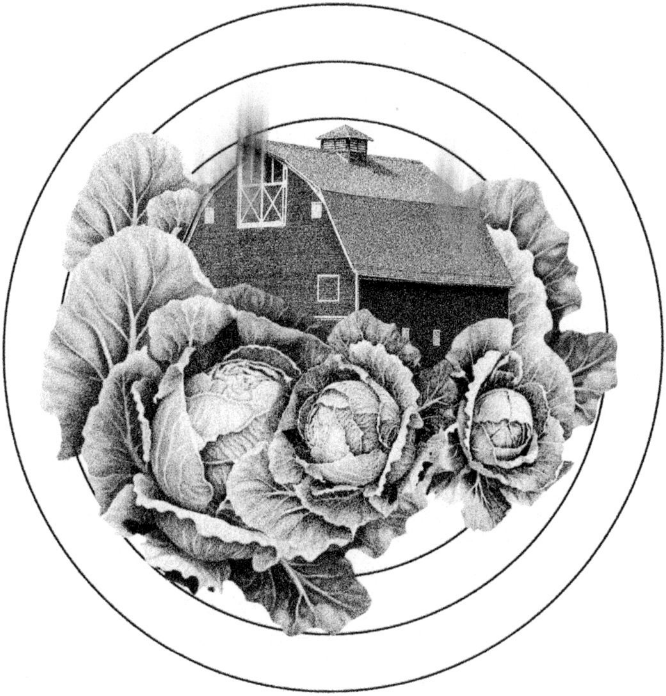

The following morning, Thomas wheeled his excited wife to the garden window so she could greet her latest blood-miracle. He opened the curtains expecting nothing more than to be greeted with absolutely nothing. Rosemary's head shot from side to side like a child outside of a toy store window. "See! I told you, Love. It was some sort of spectacle. An unexplained phenomenon."

"You mean . . . like a miracle?" Rosemary said with a smirk.

"Call it what you want; you were silly to think lightning strikes twice, or however the saying goes."

Rosemary pushed her chair away from the window and began to wheel herself toward the kitchen table for tea. Thomas could hear the disappointment in her push. "What did you wish for anyways?" He asked, trying to lighten her storm cloud.

"Doesn't matter. Do we have eggs?" Rosemary asked, a colder undertone in her words.

"I'll go and check the girls," Thomas said, putting his hat over his bald head and grabbing his small wicker basket. As the old man made his way towards the coop, he noticed that the barn door was ajar, welcoming into its chambers a small slit of daylight. This was unusual, as for fifty years the farmer had never missed a lockup. With the exception of that time long ago he'd drank one too many holiday nogs and fell asleep before dinner, only to wake up in the hay loft the following day with a pitchfork for a pillow and pants nowhere to be seen.

CABBAGE

Won't touch it to this day. Thomas hung the egg basket on the coop door to make his way over and correct his forgetfulness. As he got closer, something scoffed at him to stay back. A mystical warning from the throat of the barn, like the sound of a minotaur hiding from the light. Thomas watched as the barn doors trembled, swaying in the morning breeze. He froze, entering high alert, assessing the situation like a detective. Looking toward the door, he saw fresh scuff marks around the handle and wooden barn footing, with green stain-like scratches. Beneath his boots, indistinguishable footprints stamped throughout, with garden leaves and seeds like broken glass trailing behind like breadcrumbs.

"Hello?" Thomas called out, reaching for his pocket knife. His wife's unknown wish buzzing through his mind. The old man listened as the intruder walked back and forth in the darkness of the barn, clearly unafraid of his presence. The unknown being's confidence lowered Thomas' considerably.

"Come out you little prick; I've got a knife and I'll stab ya right in the forehead if I have to!" The old man shouted, raising his right boot and kicking open the unlatched door. Beyond the darkness stood his wife's garden wish—her blood-want appearing before his aging eyes. There was no more denying that miracles were real, which bore its own reconciliation. Now Thomas' emotions, much like a machine, had to reboot with new

CABBAGE

information as he stood at the threshold of the barn's black belly. He waved the farm dust from his vision, seeing the green between his waves. The incarnation was worse than he imagined. His brain pounding as this new reality developing before him was quickly being rewritten. His muscles went limp as he dropped the knife in disbelief, falling backward to hard dirt.

"It can't be," he managed to choke out. "It just— can't be."

The garden miracle moved into the light, illuminating every joint, limb and supernatural feature. A perennial horse made entirely of sprouts, vines and herbs. Pink radishes where eyes should have been, encased in rose petals folding with cornucopia-stocked legs and a body of cabbage shrubs. Differing shades of green draped themselves over the vegetable body, as seedlings fell from its frame with every step. The wishdream horse came close to Thomas' face, allowing the old man to smell its earthy aroma, porcini mushrooms bloomed from its pores as if it was continually growing and changing its creation and birth. The horse blew out. Its breath likened to the smell of earthworms in wet mud, shocking his system with the realization that its warmth meant it was a living being with rivering blood and air.

"What the hell are you?" Thomas whispered, raising his hands to pet the green monstrosity. The horse lowered its head, receiving Thomas's touch and pushing

CABBAGE

into his arm for more. The initial worry of danger beginning to soften, Thomas inspected the creature closer to notice he could see that right through its vegetable skeletal structure perched a pulsating, Cherokee-purple tomato for a heart. He could hear it beating with warm, green blood. Thomas picked himself up and led the horse to the large house window, where he saw Rosemary. She had been watching, as tears fell down her cheeks into her open smile. The two of them began to laugh from opposite ends of glass, Thomas petting wildly the cabbaged horse, marveling at its many parts and colors. Looking back at Rosemary, who was rushing him to come into the house with her hands.

And he knew exactly what she wanted to do.

*Spreading dark flowers,
that blossom in the night,
creating an array of colorful doom.*

Emily Slim

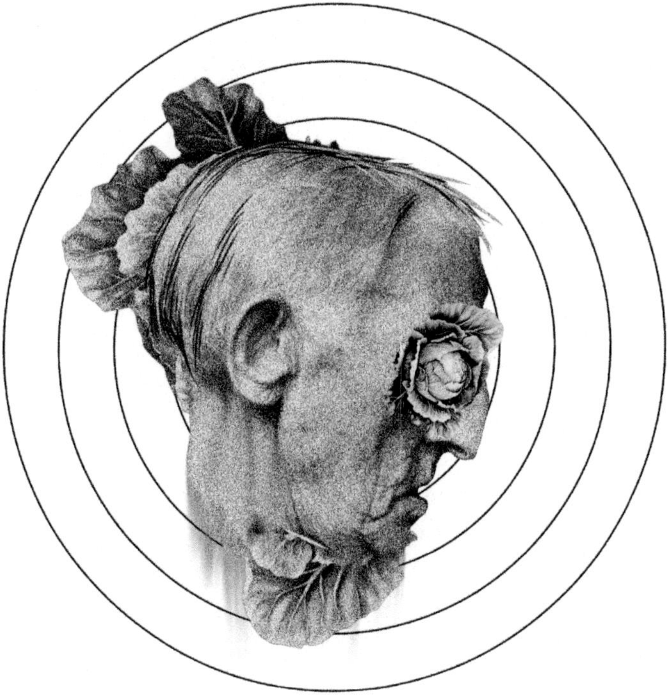

"**A**re you sure you want to do this?" Thomas asked, pouring himself another glass of red wine.

"More than anything," Rosemary said, eyes wet.

"But, Dear, this isn't a bowl of soup or a horse. We can't just tie it up in the barn."

"Exactly! It's not those things. It can be here. With us."

"But, how will we know what to do? Or how to—Last time we tried, we weren't so successful."

Rosemary pressed her frail finger against his quivering lips. "May I tell you something I've never known how to tell you?"

Thomas took a sip, coloring his lips red, and gave his wife a hesitant nod. He sat down next to her on her hospice foam bed. Readying himself for the impending sting.

"You kill the magic by always asking how, my Dear."

He took another sip, hearing and processing his dying wife's heavy accusation. He looked away from her, staring into the grandfather clock's rapid pendulum, seeing time literally slip from his grasp. He hadn't looked away from her like this since the accident. His fingers tapped the mug filled with wine, his brain chained to the gardened horse in his barn, and his fear hiding from the future. Yet, despite the fact that Thomas wanted to argue, he surrendered to her condition; a surrender to her dying wish.

CABBAGE

"I'm sorry for that," he said. "That has never been my intention. It's just after Anna . . ."

"I know," Rosemary whispered softly. "It's time to open yourself again. It's what I've been doing."

Speechless, he continued to drink his wine to avoid drinking his tears.

"When I'm gone . . ." Rosemary continued.

"Stop," Thomas said with a darkened tone. "You promised me we'd never talk like this."

"Just listen, my Love . . ." Rosemary begged, trying to de-escalate the rising tension in his voice. "*When* I'm gone, my hope is that you will abandon the word and ways of *how,* and begin to live in the mystery. This is our chance—my chance."

Thomas had a thousand concerns and even more questions as he lowered his head, removing his ragged hat. Every blood cell in his body tried to talk him out of Rosemary's wanting, but he slowly laid himself upon Rosemary's chest, letting the moment speak for itself. "There is a world wanting to give you wonder. Receive it, Thomas. I have."

Thomas wiped his eyes, and reached for the needle, "Are you ready?" He whispered.

"Bring her back to me."

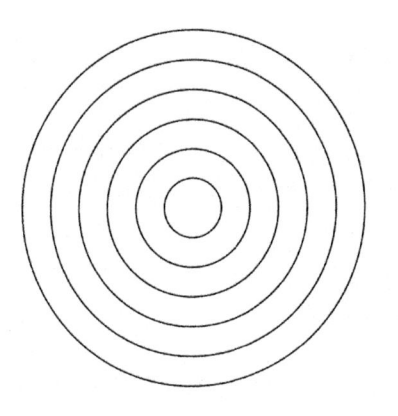

I am writing to you because I know you have a wish. I have been thinking diligently about your wish. It is not going to be easy...

Maurice Yvonne

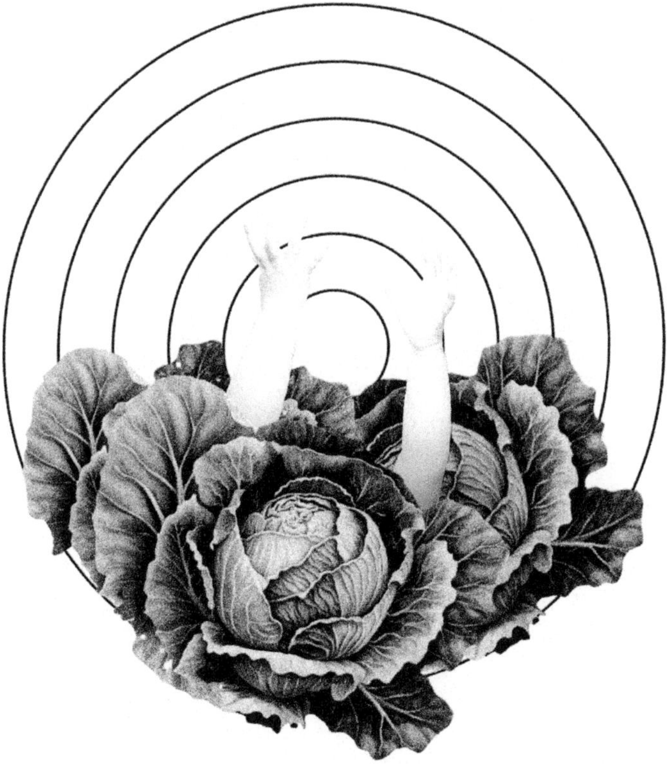

Rosemary shook her husband awake, rattling her wheelchair. Thomas had been sleeping on the couch as the medical chirps from Rosemary's machinery pecked into his slumber. "Go outside. Now!" Rosemary exclaimed.

Thomas' slow-moving mind finally caught up to the moment. "Right! Of course," he said, reaching for his hat.

"You don't have time for that! Listen!" Rosemary said, trying to pick Thomas up, elevating with what little strength she had, attempting to position him toward the window.

He stood and abruptly stopped. But it wasn't due to Rosemary's warning; it was something far more unnerving, unright, *unnatural.* Thomas watched as the curtains swayed back and forth from the morning breeze through the window, as if waving him over. *Come and see, come and behold,* he thought, watching the fabric pendulum. Beyond the confines of their humble cottage window, an infant was crying, but not just any infant . . . *their infant.* A cry so familiar, it pinched the flesh of the elderly couple inside.

"Jesus, Rosemary. It sounds like—I mean, that could be . . ." Thomas mumbled, still paralyzed in the dark room. Rosemary's hands were cupping her mouth, as her hope transfigured into reality, appeared in the form of tears and fell down her face and onto IV-scarred hands.

CABBAGE

"Go and get our daughter, Thomas." Rosemary said, with a calm authority, pushing her husband, her eyes not veering from the garden. As she knew the garden's eyes in return were fixated upon her.

Thomas did as he was told, and opened the back door as if it were the door to the underworld. The morning light broke his sight, blinding him to what lay bare in the garden beyond him. He scanned from the stairs for any sign of the infant, finally noticing the small fingers peering from cabbage leaves, like Swallowtail caterpillars. He darted forward like a bullet, "Oh God! Anna!" he shouted, nearly stumbling down the stairs as he ran toward his fresh, gardened baby.

"It can't be, it can't be, it can't be!" He cried over and over, pulling the large leaves away from the small child. Its cries softened as if she knew her father was clawing for her. Upon reaching her, he began to pull her from her garden cradle as dirt and mud caked to her back and sides, the dirty moments reminding him of Anna's birth, pulling her first from inside of her mother and now from Mother Earth. But, all at once, Thomas stepped back as he reveled at the child, while simultaneously recoiling from the sight of it.

"No . . ." Thomas whispered to the garden gods. The infant reached from beyond the green, wanting—*needing* for its caretaker. Its mossy skin, lime green, as vines sprouted from its earthy flesh-like branches. Cherry

CABBAGE

tomatoes, Fairy Tale eggplants and pink pomegranates puckered and pulsated beneath its celery stalk bones. Earthworms and yellow spiders took residence within the child like veins. Thomas' hands tremored staring at the monster, *his* monster. But nothing compared to the gardened infant's eyes . . . green carnations, unfolding from one another, flapping like monarch wings, as if blinking. Like the petal eyes knew the answers to life's worst mysteries. The moment was broken by a loud banging, as if canons blew from the barn. Thomas could see from the window the green horse kicking hard against the wall, nearly breaking the barn in half. Its screeches likened to Gorgon, blowing hard and loud. He wasn't sure, but he felt as if the horse was warning him.

Warning him that nothing about this was his once-child, though he wanted it to be. Thomas ignored the garden horse and continued to pull the baby from the earth, hearing the stems and roots crack as the ground released its miracle. Soil, leaves, ants and seeds fell from the child as he cradled the thing in his old arms. The gardened baby cooed an unnatural song, a hymn from another world—another time.

"Come to me!" Rosemary shouted from beyond the window. "Thomas, bring me my daughter!" she screamed with an electric bolt.

Thomas ran up the stairs, bringing the sunshine with him, and put their monster baby in his wife's arms, just as he had with Anna. Sweat mixed with

CABBAGE

tears cleaned the soil from his face and hands as he watched what he never thought he'd see. His daughter, or something like his daughter, alive again.

"She's perfect, she's perfect, she's mine." Rosemary cried, squeezing the green baby, mudding herself in the process.

"Rosemary, I . . . I . . ."

"Don't Thomas; we have her back."

"That's . . . I . . . How can we . . . I didn't think . . ." Thomas lost more words than his sense of the world in that moment.

Miracles were becoming common now to the elderly couple, but no one talks about what happens after the miracle breaks through. How is one supposed to drink the water of life after they've drunk the dregs of a wishing well; how does one live and breathe when monsters lay in their wife's arms?

Thomas reached for the baby, as to give his wife a minute to catch her breath.

"Don't you fucking dare!" Rosemary barked, a word Thomas had never heard her say in their lifetime.

"Rosemary?" Thomas whispered in fear, a word that nearly fell apart in his mouth.

"You don't get to *touch this* Anna, not after what happened with the last one."

Thomas took one step back, then another, standing beneath the bedroom door frame as if it were the gallows. A feeling of unwantedness broke his skin like

CABBAGE

a razor. Words he had been fearful to hear flew through the air like black moths, covering his soul in obsidian dust.

"Shut the door. Now!" Rosemary croaked loudly over the baby's unnatural noises. As Thomas slowly shut the door, he watched Rosemary lift her nightgown, exposing herself and latching the gardened child to her bare breast. Rosemary lifted her head to the heavens above and sighed. As the door came to close, Thomas could barely hear the sounds of suckling and moaning over the crack of his breaking heart.

The most painful thing is losing yourself in the process of loving someone too much...

Ernest Hemingway

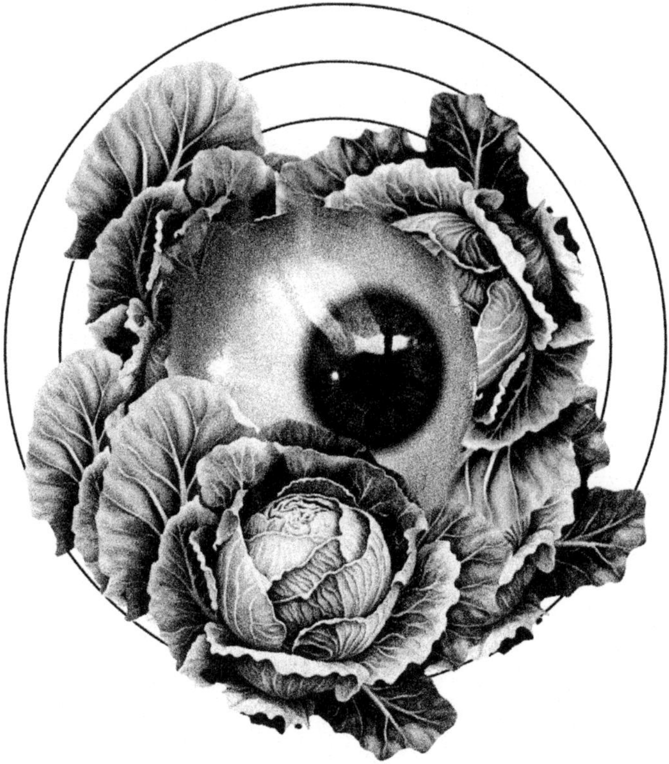

Four days had come and gone, and Rosemary and the gardened baby had not left the room. The old man wasn't sure if it was their cage, or oasis. To be with them, or to run. Nonetheless, he never ceased to knock, call for her, and pray. He'd moved the rocking chair closer to the door, listening as she talked to the child. Singing melodies that once belonged to Anna, and now to her monster. Beyond the door, the muffles gave him small moments of hope, followed by despair. As clearly as Rosemary was aware, she was uncaring toward what lay beyond her. Prepared meals next to the door's threshold began to rot, the picked daisies now wilted in the same manner as Thomas' patience. The old man lit his tenth cigarette of the evening, as night came through the house. He rocked in his chair, listening to new muffled words that brought immense dread to his failing heart.

"I'm going to make sure what happened to Anna never happens to you."

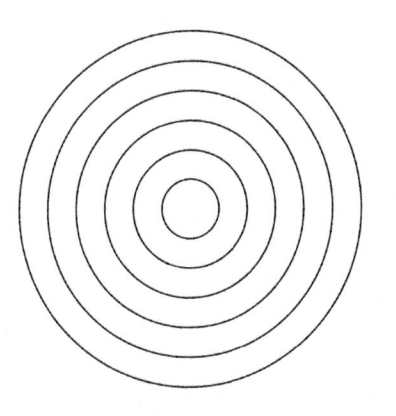

I will lend you, for a little time,
A child of mine

Edgar A. Guest

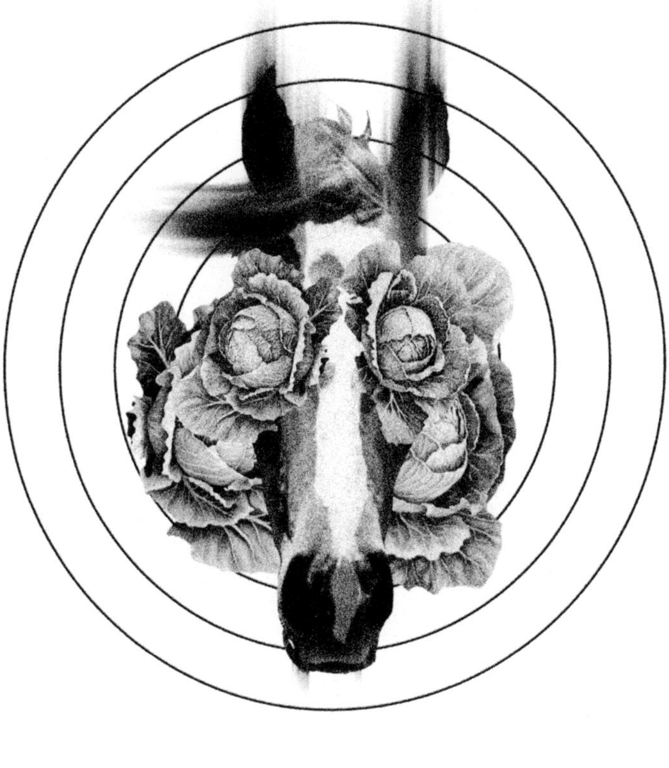

As Thomas slept in his recliner one night, he heard the ruffles of sheets and the croaking of wooden floors. His eyes worked hard to gain some composure in the darkness, and there he saw his sick wife standing against the blackness, her shadow outlined by the cold, medical equipment lights. Her silhouette in perfect stillness, as if watching her husband sleep. The image brought fear to Thomas, not hope, as the air left his body.

"Rosemary? What is it dear?" he asked nervously, noticing she was standing on her own.

"It's done," the shadow spoke back. "I'm sorry, my love."

"What? What do you mean?" Thomas said, grasping for the end table lamp.

Light swept through the room. What was intended to bring understanding only dawned greater confusion. Rosemary's gown, arms, and feet were colored in shades of red and brown. Blood and earth. Death and life.

"Rosemary, what did you do?!" Thomas asked with an unknown tone, surprising himself.

As if she didn't hear him, she turned her back on her husband, putting one hand on the wall to stabilize herself and the other to her heart. The drips of blood from her arm fell to the floor like breadcrumbs in enchanted woods, leading Thomas to the answer he was too afraid to accept.

CABBAGE

"Rosemary! What the fuck did you do?" The old man roared, making his way quickly to his leaking wife.

His heavy voice woke the green baby, who laid in its wicker basket on Rosemary's hospice bed. Thomas watched as the baby leaned itself forward, almost glaring at him with its ancient carnation eyes in . . . what was it? Judgment? Thomas could feel the green infant's disdain for him growing like a gourd.

"Ssshhh my love. You're scaring Anna," Rosemary whispered.

"That's not Anna. You know that right? That's not our daughter, Rosemary."

Rosemary whipped around to face the old man, raising her soiled and bloodied hand, and in a swift motion painted his face red. Thomas turned with the slap. "You hit me. You've never hit me." He could feel their life breaking apart in that moment and the pain of it felt a thousand hundred times worse than the pain that spread across his cheek.

"No, but I should have the day you took our Anna away."

"Rosemary! Please don't do this."

"I should have hit you a thousand times the night you let her die."

"Rosemary, don't say any more of these words, especially in your state."

"Why Thomas? Because I'm another woman you let die under your watch," Rosemary waved her hands

CABBAGE

in his face as if to brush him off, or shoo away the feelings that she'd been dying to give words to for so long.

"It was an accident, I couldn't have—" Thomas whispered.

"That's our daughter come back to us," she pointed to the bassinet. "A resurrection, and if you're too frightened to see it, to own it, then just say so." Rosemary waited for her husband's response, of which none came. "There, no more of that," she said with a final verdict. "Tomorrow, everything will be perfect."

Thomas watched Rosemary walk toward her bed, raise the green baby from its basket, and lay the child in her lap like it was the last beating heart in the universe.

C.S. FRITZ

The gentle coos of the green baby and the sounds of Rosemary's humming decades ago once brought solace, but tonight as Thomas turned out the light watching them in the dark . . . it only brought fear.

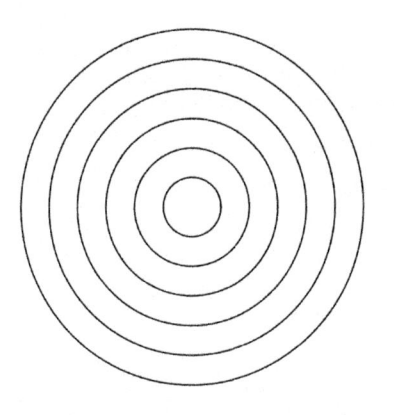

New feet within my garden go,
New fingers stir the sod;
A troubadour upon the elm
Betrays the solitude.

Emily Dickinson

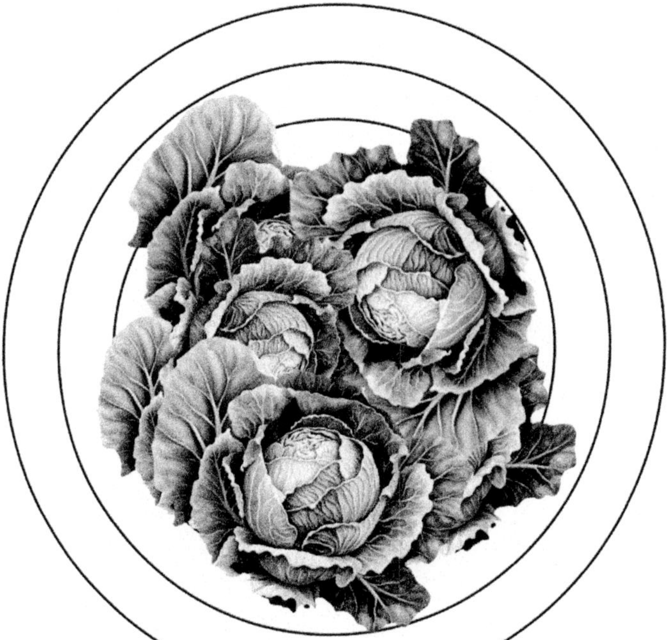

Thomas' eyes opened with the sun, remembering quickly the events of the night. His fear held him from making his way to the garden. There was no greater hell on Earth to him now than the one he planted for his wife's dying days. As he washed his wife's bloody print from his chin, watching the brown blood twirl in his sink, he felt his eyes begin to burn.

"Dammit, Rosemary," he whispered to himself. "Dammit," came again, that one more for himself; enraged for allowing all of this to transpire, entertaining Rosemary's fantasies and pain. Thomas always wanted to be stronger for her, but never knew how. Like Adam to his Eve, he allowed the serpent to win the garden.

Where are you God? he asked, a question that had never been asked before by the old man. He turned off the bathroom faucet, wiping his eyes with a warm rag, and determined what little fight he had left in himself to course correct this disaster. Rosemary was in her final days, and he wasn't going to allow himself to remember her this way. *The garden's soil has gotten in her blood, the cabbage has rotted her brain, and I will eradicate it,* Thomas thought, pushing his fist into the porcelain bathroom counter. He burst out of the bathroom door, his new plan emboldening his quest, erupting through the back door and screen. The humid day brought immediate heat to his already-soured gut, but nothing would deter him now. Thomas could see

CABBAGE

that Rosemary had been digging haphazardly the night before, as soil covered the stone pavers. Broken earth over the petals, Marigolds and Lime grass, as large mounds were erected throughout.

Jesus, Rosemary, the old man thought to himself. *What did you do?* Looking back toward the large window, he could see Rosemary watching him with the green baby in her arms. Rosemary's face was indifferent and undisturbed. As if the world's fate had already been sealed, and only she knew about it. Thomas pushed his worries aside and broke open the barn door, headed for his tool bench. There, he grabbed his fuel can and a box of matches. For the first time in days, Thomas felt a calmness wash over him and sensed a spiritual peace; something unexplainable. He was ready to burn the garden and send it back to the hell from whence it came, and he wanted Rosemary to watch. He wanted his wife to see him making a strong decision for their future and wellbeing. He wanted Rosemary to know, he was in control now, and not her. Not this fucking cabbage. Not this demonic garden. But when he exited the barn door, the window curtains were closed. In fact, every curtain and shade was sealed tightly, like the home's eyes shut in revolt. Thomas didn't know why, but he felt a pull inside. Something was wrong. His flesh and spirit torn between ending the garden's reign, and the pestilence that now plagued him to run into his

CABBAGE

home. He dropped the fuel can and matches and made haste toward the back door, "Rosemary!"

Upon entering the home, he found it black, with an unnatural musky odor to it. The only response to his frantic calls were the medical machines chirping in the distance, but they too, went quiet. Thomas felt as if all of the music of the world left him at that moment. His boots stepped heavily against the kitchen floor like military taps. But went soft as Thomas noticed the soil littered against the kitchen tile floor. Footprints.

"Rosemary?" Thomas cried out again.

She came out of the shadows, standing between slits of sunlight from the garden window. "I can't lose her again, Thomas," Rosemary whispered between gasps of air.

"Rosemary . . ."

"We've been given a gift, a gift from the gods. We need to steward it."

"Rosemary, if I promise you to look after the baby, will you please promise me that you'll listen to me?"

"Our Anna needs a full life, not like the last one. Our cabbage child needs a mother."

"Agreed my Love, you will be an amazing mother to it." A sound which broke the stagnant air brought chills down Thomas' curved spine. Rosemary laughed.

A most horrible laugh. "You think I can mother this gift from heaven? I'm dying, Thomas!"

CABBAGE

Thomas was at a loss for words, unaware of who or what his wife had become.

"Dear . . ." Thomas whispered in brokenness as he made his way to his wife. But out of the home's darkness came two more figures, stopping Thomas where he stood. Creatures from another world, revealing themselves in the partial light, their Marigold eyes illuminated in the sun slits.

"Jesus Christ, Rosemary. Come close to me! Get away from them!" Thomas exclaimed. The old man noticed that one of them was holding the green baby in its branched arms. It was then that Thomas' realization came rushing in like a warm wave, washing over his entire being, as he stared hard into his garden doppelgänger. It's pumpkin-shaped chest, pulsating and swaying between butternut lungs and green leafy flesh. His entire self, regenerated in seeds and blossoms; his blood now soil. The cabbaged beings waited patiently behind Rosemary, like angels in the throne room of God.

"We have an opportunity to give this child more than Anna had; will you join me in giving that to her? Will you join me in giving what you took away from her?" Rosemary asked, outstretching her muddied hand toward her husband.

Every nerve ending in Thomas' body raged against him for coming into this house and not burning the garden. "Rosemary," Thomas said, reaching for his wife, "I can have no more part in this charade." But, like an animal set for attack, the gardened doppelgänger

CABBAGE

lunged at Thomas, seizing his arm. Its vines twisted tightly as leaves bloomed and popped around his old skin. Thomas squealed in pain, pulling hard against them, but it was superfluous, as the more he struggled, the tighter the vines became. He watched it blink its flowered eyes with zero emotion, and pulled Thomas toward the back door. Rosemary followed slowly and steadily. He couldn't be sure, but it seemed as if she was smiling. "Rosemary! God, no! Rosemary, no!!!" Thomas shouted, breaking his voice in terror.

"Ssshhh," Rosemary said, placing her soft finger against his cracked lips. "You'll upset the baby. Soon, our Anna will have parents who can actually take care of her."

"Rosemary, please, no!"

Unhearing his pleas, she continued, "We didn't deserve Anna, and we don't deserve this baby. This is our sacrifice, our punishment."

"Rosemary, I beg of you!" the old man pleaded, "I'm not ready to die, I'm not ready, I'm not ready, I'm not ready!" The old man screamed, as the green demons continued to drag Thomas out and to the garden. The very hell he planted. Between Thomas' cries for help, the green infant had awoken as well, crying out for its mother. The world stood silent to watch. Thomas, looking upward, unable to move, could see differing birds perched on the roof of the house as witness, as the wild flowers aimed their blossoms toward the moment.

One final plea to his wife: "Rosemary, I don't want to die."

CABBAGE

"Neither did Anna, but now we can go to her," Rosemary said, as Thomas watched her step gingerly into a freshly dug grave. "I'll see you soon, my Love," she said calmly, with finality. She blew him a kiss from soiled hands, spraying blood and black dirt.

"Rosemary! No!!!" Thomas screamed, as his gardened self let him fall onto his back against the cold wet soil. He dug his fingers into the fresh, black walls that made up the casket. "I'm not ready to die!" the old man screamed to the sun above, repeating it over and over again for God to hear. Tears and snot washed the dirt from his fearful face. "Oh God, please please please, I'm not ready." Soon, soil rain began to shower upon him, as the gardened doppelgängers began to refill the coffins they had dug. Thomas' pleading was soon muffled by the very dirt he planted only months before. Tasting it, eating it, choking on it, breaking beneath it. Their lives, like seeds in the garden soil, soon to break apart and bless the earth.

Does the seed know it must die?

Does the seed know that with the springing forth of every wild rose, the seed in the earth must first die? Crushed by its own purpose for life to blossom. But does the seed have a choice? Does the earth ever pardon it? Does the black dirt cry or feel remorse?

This is what garden soil longs to do, to break and bless the ground. To fill the green world with fresh color. Resurrecting shades of dragon pink and angel blue . . . but does the seed know this?

Do you?

ALBATROSS BOOK CO.

Albatross Book Co. is a book craft and boutique publishing house.
We are a one stop shop for all your needs to make your book a reality.

albatrossbookco.com

Other recent published works include:

SOON TO BE A MAJOR MOTION PICTURE!

A Fig For All the Devils

An abused, grief-stricken, and impoverished Sonny has all but given up on life. That is, until he meets death, by way of the Grim Reaper. The Reaper, a junk food loving, poetry reading, cigarette-addicted entity, has no time to waste as he searches for a suitable successor who would become "Death" for the next millennium. By training the boy in the ways of death and dying, Reaper grooms his young apprentice and through suspenseful and horror-laced events, he unknowingly gives Sonny something he never intended:
A reason to live.

WINNER OF BEST IN HORROR

Other recent published works include:

ALL CREATURES LIVING BENEATH THE SUN

Most are familiar with the legend of the Pied Piper of Hamelin, but few of know of the lore that surrounds it.

This harrowing myth tells of a mysterious piper who lured the town's children away, never to be seen again.

All except three.

One blind, one lame and one deaf.

This is their violent, brutal, grotesque, disturbing and heartwarming story.

Printed in Great Britain
by Amazon